# All the Things I Love About You

written and illustrated by

## LeUyen Pham

BALZER + BRAY
*An Imprint of HarperCollinsPublishers*

Balzer + Bray is an imprint of HarperCollins Publishers.

All the Things I Love About You
Copyright © 2010 by LeUyen Pham  All rights reserved.
Manufactured in China. No part of this book may be used or reproduced in any manner whatsoever
without written permission except in the case of brief quotations embodied in critical articles and
reviews. For information address HarperCollins Children's Books, a division of
HarperCollins Publishers, 10 East 53rd Street, New York, NY 10022.
www.harpercollinschildrens.com

Library of Congress Cataloging-in-Publication Data is available.
ISBN 978-0-06-199029-8

10 11 12 13 14   SCP   10 9 8 7 6 5 4 3 2 1

❖

First Edition

For all those many mamas
who love their little boys,
this book is just for you.

There are oh so many things
I love about you.

I love

the way your hair
looks in the morning.

I love

how you look
in pajamas.

Although getting you out of them
is another story.

I love . . .

how you eat.

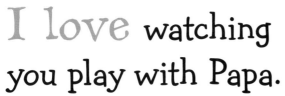

I love watching
you play with Papa.

Sometimes.

I love the feel
of your heartbeat

as if you have a butterfly
fluttering in your insides.

I love
when you hug me
like this . . .

. . . and like this . . .

. . . and especially like this!

I love how you skip the letter "Y"
in the alphabet because

is so much fun to say.

I love hearing
you say

MAMA!

Although sometimes
I prefer "Papa."

I love when you hold my hand.

And even when you let go . . .
I know I haven't.

And I *oh so love* hearing you laugh.

I love

how every day
  you grow just
    a little more . . .

. . . how every day you learn
just one more new thing.

And when I think
I can't possibly
love you any more,

the next moment I do.

There are so many things I love about you.
But mostly, I just love . . .
*you.*